Women Rock
A Collection of Short Erotica F/F Stories

Includes:

Seducing the Boss
Erica's Dilemma
Hot Desking I & II
Christmas Menage

by C. J. Starr

Women Rock: A Collection of Short Erotica F/F Stories
Copyright 2012 C. J. Starr
ISBN 978-1-61829-055-7

Published by New Line Press

Dedicated to my girlfriends

Table of Contents

Seducing the Boss..1

Preface 3

Chapter One 5

Chapter Two..11

Chapter Three 15

Chapter Four 17

Chapter Five 23

Erica's Dilemma 27

Chapter One 29

Chapter Two..33

Chapter Three 35

Hot Desking Stories 41

Hot Desking I...43

Hot Desking II 51

Christmas Menage..63

Chapter One 65

Epilogue 75

A Special Note from C. J. Starr 77

About the Author 79

List of City Girl Series...81

Seducing the Boss

Preface

My name is Taylor, Taylor O. Blake; the "O" ac-cording to my ex-boyfriend stands for oversexed. Now, with that little tidbit aside, I'm compelled to tell you my personal inside story. A true tale of how a little bit of sexual promis-cuity, straight or gay, can change one's life -- forever. This all happened – only one week ago. And now, without guilt, without shame, and without consequence from God or any living human being -- my story now unfolds...

Chapter One

It was a warm June evening. A Friday night, and I found myself home...alone, again. My boyfriend, Richard, was away on business, a trip to France. He travels there, to Champagne, often, on behalf of his company, "Wines of Europe," as a buyer in the wine import industry. And me, I work 9-5 as a web-advertising consultant. Basically, I purchase ad spots for start-up businesses.

My boss, Sally Anderson, treats me like a genuine goddess, and I – well, I've secretly fallen in love with her. For years, I've looked at her with a seductive eye and yet, somehow, I've controlled my deeply hidden sexual wants and desires for her. Mostly by satisfying my latent and ever festering carnal needs for her -- through my lover, Richard. How many nights I had lain at his side and pretended that he, muscle building Richard, was my Sally with her soft and plushy breast snuggled up warm and tight against me.

I found many ways to stop myself from seducing her, ways to control my urges to be intimate with her. Oh, I've felt these feelings before, with others, but this was a whole new chemistry that enveloped me toward Sally and it was simply maddening. My boss, my beloved, was just too damned straight!

Turning off the TV, I went to my bedroom and stripped naked. I stood looking at myself in an old antique full-length mirror. I liked what I saw. My breasts were firm and, I must say, well naturally proportioned. As I ran my hands over them – my nipples responded and formed a pair of dark magenta thimbles that poked up from the aureole centers; a small mystery this wee formation, one that still amuses me when they are touched or kissed or suckled upon.

Turning my butt to the glass, I looked over my shoulder and studied my ass. This pleasant view convinced me that my exercise routines were worth all the time and effort that I spent to keep myself nicely contoured. I could see that my flesh was firm and totally cellulite free. Yes, firm but my skin felt soft and oh so smooth to my own touch. I let my hands press gently around the silky cheeks and it felt nice, very nice. I felt a small pang of arousal and that too was nice.

I turned back and eyed myself further fixating on my tummy; I'm an inny and a cute inny as far as navels go... My hands toured my hips and then I focused on my pubic patch of auburn strands and felt the hairs playfully with my fingertips. I begin fondling my pussy mound as I watched, amused, and thoughtless of what I was doing and of my immediate surroundings. With both hands I exposed the pink flesh of my clitoral appendage, and then a euphoric wave of pleasure engulfed my senses as I made little light circles around my now fully extended clitoris.

Moisture developed as my fingers toyed in with gentle, and deliberate, sensitive, plunges between the folds of my titillated flesh. A heavy breath, my own, and a deep inhale had signaled my increasing passion to reach self-gratification. And my thoughts took off on an instant excursion to a mental picture of my latest friend and lover, Richard. Rich, with his chiseled facial features now hovered flush over my upward gyrating, grinding pussy, his mouth suckled gently all around and everywhere about my clitoris and then he lapped his tongue in tempo to my quickening fevered pitch and to his own orgasmic-prompted oral madness.

And then he'd stop ever so briefly. He'd softly whisper to me how, superb, my juices tasted. Then, with those soft, but exacting, echoes of past lovemaking racing through my head, I swiped my own two middle fingers deep and firm up into my moistened vagina and retracted them, wet, covered deliciously with my own sticky love serum. Then placed them, one by one, hungrily into my trembling mouth where I licked each of them to a tasty and hygienic cleanliness, and then reached down for yet more.

Euphoric, I moved to the bed and sprawled out with my legs spread open and my knees elevated and I thought more on how Richard had these special ways -- with his mouth -- that no man (or woman) before or after him could ever come close to matching. His skill, his timing, and the amount of pressure that he applied were always measured and always just beyond that cutting edge of giving pleasure as an act of perfection. His sexual game was to please and, I'm here to attest, he always won! I always let him...

I softly gripped my pussy and made my Mound de Venus flesh move in a circular direction. With my other hand stroking lightly across my breasts and down the length of my tanned torso and then back up, over and over again and again in rapid movements that fired my skin to new highs of self-indulgent pleasure. And then -- with an uncontrolled and sudden spasm, my body arched upward and my thighs tightened about my hand and an unearthly euphoria permeated through every cell of my incarnate being. An uncontrollable scream rose unbridled from the depths of my satisfaction center, up and out it came -- a cry of pure fulfilled lust and uninhibited jubilation.

And then this strange feeling, a passion, overwhelmed me, and a three-dimensional vision of my co-worker, Sally (Sunshine) Peterson enveloped my every throbbing sense. She was naked before me and she – seemed -- so very, very real. I reached the light on the nightstand and turned it on. The vision ended. My God! My boss appearing to me nude and in an erotic pose of touch me, feel me, see me...and with that flash of light, the vision was dispelled. All of that beautiful vividness out of my, what should have been -- sexually satiated mind.

I laughed to myself and then questioned my own sexual orientation. Why was I seeing, imagining, my best friend Sally? Naked! I just didn't have an answer. But as I thought a little deeper on it, I came up with a few plausible and completely pleasurable ideas.

Sal is a naturally sexy woman. She dresses like a 200-dollar hooker and always smells like a 500-dollar whore. She's married to a genuine hunk, James, a guy so suave he sends her a flower every day of the goddamned week. And when he visits our office, it's always, "My little bird." Or "Baby Sweets." Or he'll walk in and kiss her full on the mouth – too long, and he rubs her ass right in front of my face, that bastard.

One day, she, Sally, actually asked if I'd go somewhere for twenty-minutes so she could give sweetie a quick blowjob. And me, I left... Now, who's the fool on that one? So. I deliberately came back in ten minutes, and I caught her, on her knees, and him all smiles zipping up his pants like nothing had ever happened. So, James says to me, quietly so Sal can't hear, "What? You never sucked a dick during business hours?" Then he smiles a sick smile and walks out; leaving me red-faced in front of Sal.

Sal heard, even though she wasn't supposed to. She says to me, "I'm glad you came back early, Taylor. Another minute and he'd have shot his wad and... I would have had to swallow. We're out of Kleenex," she said, smiling through her slightly swollen lips. But even that, she did with élan. Brushed it off as an office chore and goes right back to being pretty and proudly taking care of business.

Oh! ...I had read a copy of Playboy, one that Richard had left lying around, this was earlier that evening, too. That, coupled with the fact that Richard was on an extended stay over in France for the last three weeks and not due back for another two... Well, maybe – just maybe, I do hold some latent lesbian desires, especially for Sal.

Okay! I do hold these strange feelings. And at that very moment, I turned off the bed-lamp and fell back down on my green silk designer sheets. Naked, with my hand resting loosely atop my still vibrant pussy, I regained my vision of Sally kneeling above my face. I closed my eyes with the picture of her clit exposed above me and I swear it literally made my mouth water. The last waking thought that I held that night was, "I have to seduce Sally... I will seduce Sally – Cum on, Monday morning."

Chapter Two

When I woke on Saturday, I had slept in until 9 a.m., I felt fresh and then recalled dreaming of Richard. His penis was exposed to me sticking out of the zipper hole of his pants. It was erect and oh so hard. The purple tip had a single drop of oozed semen protruding from his little penis hole. I tried to move forward to lick it away, but every time I did, it would retract back, all the way back, right into his pants. When I'd withdraw from my attempt, the penis would come out again. This went on as a recurring sequence until I finally lunged forward and caught his shiny bulb in my drooling lips. I sucked around the head and tasted the salty excretion on my taste buds. Oh my God, it was so titillating! I engulfed him as deep as I could and took over half of his cock full into my mouth.

He began to throb -- his penis began to throb, full out as I clamped down on his ready to ejaculate peter head and rolled my tongue over his, now gushing, sperm. And he did, he exploded full into my ready and willing mouth. And then, the dream changed!

Richard's penis became Sally's clitoris, and her beautiful juices poured out into my mouth and oozed down my chin, to my neck, and down onto the silk bedding. There was so much! And it tasted so wonderfully delicious. I pulled her tight against my face and went into orgasm on my own -- without even being touched. And then, I woke...

I had actually drooled in my sleep. Something I never do. I looked at my pillows and at the damp sheets and began laughing. Jesus Christ! I even looked to see if Sally was indeed in my bed – hiding under my covers. The dream was that vivid! I lay there in a slight post-orgasmatic pant. I relived the dream several more times; until it vanished from my cognizant, short memory. Parts of the dream still lingered: Richard's beautiful prick and the sheen of its tight bulbous tip; that tasty lone drop of his semen; and the cum explosion into my wanton mouth... But the best part, Sally's clit between my lips – well, I have that part locked in my long-term memory now. I have recalled that fantastic scene a hundred times since then, and I'm sure I'll go there often in the future, Yes, as a recollection worth a million dollars... Ah, such a tasty, tasty dream.

The sheets had to be changed and the pillowcases, too. But it was all worth it. I headed for the shower still vibrant and, yes! Damp between my legs, too.

I took a long soaking shower. I soaped my breasts in a fondling zest. I was feeling so alive just thinking of Sally. But, when I lathered my pussy with my scented soap bar, my thoughts turned to Richard and his nine-inch penis.

Dragging the cake of soap slowly across my pelvis, I wished it were Richard's stiffness and not a bar of scented soap. I remember talking to the soap, "How'd that feel, Mister Bubbles?" and I laughed. And actually had a pang, an erotic pulse, which shot up my newly lubricated vagina. I moved Mister Bubbles to my ass and smeared the softening bar up my crack, twisting the soap a bit, getting the bar's edge slightly up my hole and then – massaged there with my fingertips.

This felt pleasant and with the soap as a lubricant I entered myself for a brief moment of anal arousal. It was nice. It made me recall the first time that Richard fucked me in the ass. I was afraid, then. Yet – I found myself enjoying his sexual perversion. But, no pun intended, I no longer view this ass-act as being so perverse, it's just a little bit -- unconventional?

I spread my legs in a slight squat and turned the showerhead to pulse and let the water jets rinse about my pelvis. It felt so nice, so warm... I let the water beat against my thighs and made circular moves with the head and the contoured molding of the flexible spray nozzle. My thoughts raced to Sally's beautiful mouth and I pretended that the pressure I felt was from her lips caressing my labia and teasing my exposed, and now, highly sensitive clitoris, and I did this -- right into orgasm. Damn! It felt so powerful, so sexually rewarding, and I stayed there until the water no longer ran warm and I only turned off the faucet when I felt a slight shiver from the cold – cold water.

Dab drying with an ultra-soft cotton towel I seriously wondered if Sally would, indeed, succumb to my sexual advances. I wanted her. I wanted to touch her. I wanted to lock lips, and dart my tongue into her mouth. I wanted her to be responsive to my fondling of her breasts and my gripping her gorgeous ass. I wanted to hear her moan as I pulled on her clitoris with my lips and feel her tremor with delight as I ran the tip of my tongue back and forth across her ass hole while grasping her firm ass with one hand and delving into her pussy with the other – I wanted her to scream! To scream out in an esoteric freedom of pleasurable delight, to scream out from every gentle touch of my feminine hands and every one of my pampering finger manipulations. And I had to squeeze my thighs together on these pleasurable thoughts that had encompassed me. As I dried, out loud, and for my own benefit, I sang out, "I am going to fuck you, Sally! And I'm going to enjoy every fucking moment of it."

Chapter Three

My masturbating had left me tender around the outer fringes of my pussy. My clitoris was overworked to the point that my touching it was no longer a pleasure. I laughed at my own foolishness as I was still in a desirous mood, a mood to experience more physical arousal – I was in that numb state of mentally wanting, needing, to have further sexual feelings expressed -- the pleasure of satisfaction, and having it right then -- all by myself.

I applied a soothing gel, a new skin softener, one that came in a penis-sized applicator. The blue translucent cream turned invisible upon contact with my flesh. The effect of the wintergreen scent and the tingling, soothing, properties of the product immediately eased the soreness that I was, up to then, unfortunately experiencing.

Climbing into bed with the gel tube in hand, just in case, I fluffed my pillows and snuggled in for a restful sleep. And I did sleep -- deep and sound. And I dreamt...

Richard was in my office. He was seducing Sally on top of Sal's desk while I worked on a monthly statistical report, junk for posterity. I tried to ignore their brash display but they kept looking at me to ensure that I was taking in every one of their grunts and groans. And then Sally's husband walks in.

He comes walking across the floor and right up to my desk and whispers to me, while pointing a thumb toward Richard and Sally, "What's that all about, Taylor?" and he has this big smile glued across his face and he was more concerned with observing my cleavage than challenging his wife as to why she was madly fucking my boyfriend's brains out right there in the office.

And then I'm walking hand in hand with James toward Sally's desk. Richard's bare ass is rising and falling as he pumps hard and sweaty into Sally who is observing our approach with a snickering grin that is at the same time issuing audible grunts in tune to Richard's plunges.

James reaches out his hand and places it on Richard's tightened butt and pats it, saying, "Slow down there my boy, slow down." as we stood alongside the desk still holding hands and just watched. Then Sally claws Richard's back in a frenzied display of orgasmatic pleasure that shoots through her now taught torso. Her face contorts in a pleasure-scream and is then joined instantly with the voice of Richard extolling his own orgasmatic expletives to his own God as some form of thank you to his own asexual universe and his own moment of pure and unadulterated male ecstasy.

The dream ends with me rubbing Sally's pussy, smearing all the shared jissum that they exuded so methodically and jointly, into, over, and all around her bushy and now gooey blonde pussy hair. And then I woke. And... Saturday was upon the dawn and I didn't find my tube of ointment until I entered the confines of my shower and there it was, by golly. This gave me a hearty laugh as I extracted the comforting penis form from between my still tender labia lips. And it made me laugh.

Chapter Four

Richard called me from Europe. I had just finished blow-drying my hair after that leisurely morning shower. There I stood, naked, chit chatting with the blower in one hand and my cell in the other. He said he was just going to bed. It was late there, in Champagne, and he complained that he had tasted way too many samples of the local wines. And then, I heard a faint giggle in the background.

"Richard, is there someone with you?"

"Don't be silly, sweetheart. No. There isn't anyone here but me."

"There damn well better not be, Richard." and before I could finish, the line went dead. "Richard! Richard? Are you there, baby?"

Needless to say, that little conversation started my day off on a very sour note. That bastard was with another woman! It really pissed me off, too. He was only gone for two, three weeks and he couldn't keep his dick holstered for a mere fourteen more days. Damn him! Frustrated, I finished drying my hair with a full-blown fury. Something was going on in France. Richard was fucking around. I distinctly heard the background giggles. And, I just wasn't buying the snap disconnection. Why do men have to be like this? He has such a beautiful, intelligent, and outgoing woman — me. Yet he's going to go over there and fuck around. I was working up a jealous streak and it was becoming quite maddening.

* * *

An aside... During Richard's stateside call to Taylor, a fourteen-year-old French hussy, one that claimed to be eighteen, was sucking off Richard's nine-inch penis. As she poked a finger full up Richard's ass she simultaneously grasped his balls with her other hand. The consequence was a premature orgasm smack into her un-expecting youthful mouth. This happened at the exact moment that Richard had to sever his oversea connection. Yes. Had to!

Mimi laughed aloud as his cum ran down her chin and began a thick milky coating on her tiny, but well formed, teenage breasts. Mimi had never experienced such a copious flow from any of her Parisian boyfriends. With excitement, she then proceeded to suck up every last explosive drop of Dick's still warm and saline laced cum. This was all happening about the time his cell phone lid was excitedly snapped down to sever their connection. Richard yelled out in climax, American style, "Oh, God damn, Mimi!" so loud, that management was called to his room to investigate a domestic violence call; one that was made to the hotel's desk clerk shortly after Richard climaxed.

Mimi was excited. Ha! She was exuberant, with her juvenile adventure. She immediately insisted that she give Dick a second, consecutive, orgasm via her talented tongue and her manipulative handwork. To which -- Richard had readily and greedily agreed.

Several minutes later, when management entered without knocking, Richard went into climax, again, for the second time. Mimi in a dreamy trance of pure pleasure, heard the entry and looked to the door... With cum oozing from her slightly swollen lips, she, gagging, exclaimed, "Papa!"

The American Embassy is trying to get Richard back to the states as this is being written. Poor Richard...

* * *

Angry and frustrated by Richard's call, I dressed comfy in a light skirt and a deep V-neck top. Deliberately, I abandoned my panties and it made me feel sexy beyond all get-outs. Some lucky guy was going to get an eyeful somewhere along the line, and I promised myself that it wouldn't be a simple accident. Then, in the same breath, I added, "Fuck you Richard." And then thought about Sally, my lovely, beautiful Sally.

On the way downtown, I was cognizant of the leather seat grasping my ass. I wished it was Sally and in the windshield, I envisioned her undressed and allowing me to suck her breasts and let me kiss up and down her flat tummy and letting me dart my tongue into her delta of honey sweetened oozing pussy flesh. And a horn blared loudly as a huge delivery truck came up along side of my passenger door. The driver was grinning like a hog in an apple patch as he loomed at my crotch with bugged-out eyes. My hand was up my skirt and it made me happy that the fat-fuck driver had noticed. I smiled and winked over in the trucks direction. Then, I slowed and deliberately allowed him to pass.

Regaining the image of Sally in my minds eye, I knelt before her – gripping her ass, I pulled her pussy into my wanton lips, and I swear, my mouth watered, and I literally darted out my tongue to enter her juicy portal of pleasure. But the light turned yellow ahead of me and the thoughts – so beautiful as they were – vanished into the reality of heavy traffic and the need to drive safe.

Two blocks later, I was at Flassiddio's Dress Shoppe, a high-end shop where all the swanky hookers buy their toxic street wear, the clothes that make a man go erect before he even notices that you have a really fine ass and serious cleavage, a cleavage that makes a man want to go deeper than the bottom of the Grand Canyon itself.

It was ten-o-clock sharp, they had just opened, and a young girl asked me if I needed assistance. She was so damned cute, Jesus! I thought, "Yes! Honey baby, you could assist me, right into an orgasm, by my just looking at you."

Recklessly, looking at her seductive curves that were all amply exposed by a watermelon colored outfit, I asked if she'd show me something like the whore dress she was personally wearing. And then – to my own surprise, I reached out and touched the cloth that enwrapped her plush, and openly exhibited erect nipples, breasts, and inquired, "Silk?"

Smiling playfully, ignoring my touch to her top, she eyed me from head to toe. "Yes, it's silk. I just love it." and then she quickly suggested, "It comes in several colors, and I'm sure we have a size six. You are a size six, aren't you?"

"Yes. A sex. I mean, six." And then I found myself saying, "You are a very beautiful young woman." I reached the hem of her short skirt and grasping it, I felt the material, also a silk but not a real glossy one. I slightly lifted the hem and as I did so I felt this wonderful rush of blood flush up to my face – I had observed that Little Miss Big Tits wasn't wearing any panties either, and I swear, she had a hopeful shadow of lust flash across her face when I looked up at her. She allowed herself to turn dreamy eyed, and then her powder blue eyes gave it all up, as she squinted with an accepted knowledge of her own need. And we both smiled. And in that quick but deep moment of stark wonderment -- we both knew.

She helped me strip naked in the four-mirror fitting-room. She then ordered me (very dyke like) to sit on the padded bench. To which, I gladly and oh so willingly, did. I had already succumbed to her dominance, I was now her bitch, and I'd do anything and everything she wished. It wasn't discussed, it wasn't negotiated, it was intuitive and I wanted it, badly, and went with the mystery.

Her silk hit the floor, floated to the floor, like the parachute material that it was and exposed the most beautiful pussy that I had ever seen, anywhere, and I had spent some nice time viewing pussy on the Internet.

She moved into my face and I took her hungrily between my lips. She grabbed my hair and guided my head forcefully, but gently flush, against her gyrating hips. She then lifted a leg to the bench to give her pussy more space and my tongue a clearer entry. And she poured, sakes alive she spewed, love juices almost faster than I could swallow, it was so delicious! She was unbelievably – aah, was just dripping fantastic. I dug my nails into her butt and pulled her tight and I felt her shake in the bold tremors of an unstoppable orgasm. It made me feel so alive to be giving her such a powerful and unabashed release.

She put her leg down and we kissed magnificent kisses as she fondled my breast and hardened up my nipples. Then, she ordered me to bend over the bench and offer up my ass -- to her mouth. And – Oh my God! She had her head flush full against my ass and her tongue was entering my asses hole with the fastest in and out movement that I never thought was humanly possible.

Then, while tonguing me, she reaches around and grabs my entire pelvic area and starts this tender grind with both hands. I knew I was soaking her hands in natural lubricants and it felt so fucking wonderful – I wanted to just scream. She then ran one hand up and down my tummy and I just exploded in horrific ecstasy. I mean – I saw stars! I saw rainbows. I shot right up through the entire Milky Way's milk and landed smack dab back down on Venus. And we kissed again, deep and hungry, and she smiled a knowing smile that she had reciprocated beyond all belief the pleasures that I had just extended onto her. And we dressed, and I purchased a cream-colored-silk-whore's-outfit for four hundred dollars.

As I staggered out to my Lexus I felt a secondary shudder of continuing orgasmic, after shocks! I placed the pink shopping bag on the passenger's seat and then stared at the clerk's home phone number, the only thing that she quickly scrawled on back of the store's business card. I never asked her for her name. It simply hadn't come up. But, I had her number... And as I pulled out of the parking lot, I noticed her waving at me from behind the store's mauve tinted window. As I pulled into my driveway, still vibrant from my nips to my clit, I recall, saying this out loud, "Fuck you Richard! You've been replaced, Mister Dick."

Wearing my new outfit, I inspected my new image in the full-length mirror. I was hot. The skimpy dress made me look like I was ready for anything; as long as it was sexual.

And then I pretended that I was Sally looking at me, Taylor, and I thought, how could Sally not want to have sex with me? It was a sure thing; we were as good as in bed, almost. "Hurry Monday!" was now my battle cry. I would seduce her and life would be beautiful – forever.

Chapter Five

I spent all day Sunday healing all the tender spots of my sexual being. I worked in the garden and pulled every weed that showed its ugly self. I pondered Richard with disdain; every thought I ever had of marrying him was being thrown out now; along with my pile of discarded weeds.

About eight that night I took a long, soothing, scented bath. I would smell like a jasmine forest come morning, and I'd be as clean as a kitchen plate fresh out of the dishwasher, just for Sally's pleasure. As I soaked, I practiced mentally how I'd approach her. It would work. It had to work! My love was too strong for it not to work. And then I crawled into bed. I began to contemplate what had happened at Flassiddio's.

The Shoppe, the fitting room, and 555-6969 aroused me. Just thinking about it made me warm, made me glow with passion. Suddenly, I was masturbating with my nightstand adjunct, my vibrator (I have named it, Mickey). And I fell asleep with the damn thing buzzing away against my clitoris.

Monday morning arrived; I dressed to the nines, dabbed on my best (90 dollar an ounce) scent, fluffed up my hair, and headed for my destiny – Sally. The new outfit felt great and it made me feel like a million bucks. I wore my beige sandals with the narrow heel strap and weaved open toes; because, they kick off very nicely. I was all set. I matched; and I knew that I was an icon of pure sexuality.

Sally's car, a gun barrel-blue Mercedes convertible, was already in the lot when I arrived. The top was down and I thought this a good thing as a sign of her free-spirited nature. I parked my silver Lexus next to hers as a personal display of coziness. Then -- with all the confidence of a Chief Justice, I entered the office.

Sally was seated at her desk drinking a carried in Star-bucks coffee, the Monday Morning Moocow, as we had come to call it. Mine was ready on my desk. Sally always bought on Mondays; it was ritualistic.

My dress was noticed immediately, "Wow! Look at you, Taylor. Have a date after work? I thought Richard was out of town?"

I braved myself and boldly stated, "I dressed up for you, Sal." I walked to her desk and modeled my wares, "Do you like?"

Sal removed her reading glasses and took a hard look at what I was offering. She had a coy smile form on her lips and just froze there and ogled me. And I knew I felt her seeing me as an available sexual entity. It sent me into a breathing pant, a pant of desire. I felt like a wild animal, a panther in heat waiting to mate, instantly, right there, right on the jungle's floor.

I blurted out, "I love you Sally."

Sally's mouth opened very slightly. She was about to say something, something wonderful! But nothing came out of her mouth, no words. Nada! Nothing... She just stared at me with her beautiful mouth hanging wide open and looking so damn gorgeous.

Tears began to well up in my eyes; I stammered out the words, "I want...to ...make love with you, Sal."

* * *

Everything after that was pandemonium. Expletives flew out of Sal's mouth like machine gun bullets. Words about the wrath of hell echoed around the office walls and probably still are, as I sit here and write this down, today. I was then fired, right on the spot. Those horrible words "Get out! And don't you ever come back." are now etched into my brain for the rest of eternity.

I passed James on his way in as I made my last trip out from loading my personal things into my car. Sally had called him to come to her side. I remember his last word, the one he foolishly said to me, "ARF!" That was the ugly bastard's only remark. I think he was just imitating himself, as a mad dog, in animalistic heat.

On Tuesday, I called the 555-6969 number and asked if there were any job openings. There were. On Wednesday, I interviewed extensively -- in the fitting room. On Thursday, I was officially hired after answering a few follow up questions, which were presented, in the fitting room. On Friday, I worked my first day with Barbara, my brand new boss and (of course) my newest lover.

Erica's Dilemma

Chapter One

My name is C. J. Starr and I have a new story to relate. As most of you already know, I write somewhat unusual stories with a strong sexual base. Many of my contemporary authors refuse to pen what goes on in the world around us, sexually, and leave these insights to the reader's imagination. Oh, we all know what goes on -- but there is an odd aversion, a downright taboo, to being too graphic about love, about commingling, and the open act of sex -- in general.

Well, I am going to call an orgasm, an orgasm and a penis, a penis in this recantation.

Although I'm not known to be a switch-hitter, this story was revealed to me during a romantic evening with a dear friend of mine named, Erica.

Yes, we licked each other's pussy and we both had a sensuous night playing around on a silk-sheeted king-sized bed at a friend's place up on Lake Tahoe. It was a fun and reckless night and I'd be quite ready to experience that night all over again (a public acknowledgement to Erica) at the drop of a proverbial cowboy hat.

With Erica's help, I will pen her amazing tale of an unusually sexual night with three sexually motivated young men. So...let me start at the beginning.

I had my hands firmly on Erica's butt, pulling her pelvis gently against my mouth. My tongue was darting rapidly into her moist vagina when she went into an unbelievably, intense -- body stiffening -- orgasm.

Erica screamed out, "My God, C. J., I'm letting go!" and she did, and I knew she entered that mystical world of climax with a total loss of mental, worldly cognizance. There was a delicious rush of her sweet tasting juices. An exotic gush spewed forth, a liquid torrent of lust; it filled my mouth and threw me into an immediate, joint and mutual, orgasm.

It was an exhilarating moment for me. I normally experience my orgasm(s)...usually multiple, before the man has his. With that aside, and with me being engrossed in my own orgiastic fury, that's when Erica began panting out her story.

"I haven't...felt like this... Since...those three boys...took me along...on their... Bachelor party. Oh my God! You are too much, C. J."

"Three! Tell me about it, Erica." I asked as I hovered above her and moved my licking up to her enlivened, taut nipples.

"Oh C. J.," she cooed. "It was last year. I had just met this hunk down in LA."

Talking into her breast, I insisted she relate her story to me, "Tell me all about it, every detail, Erica." as I continued masticating on her breasts; Erica's skin is so beautiful, I was ready to lick her to death, or at least into another orgasm.

"I was down in Anaheim and his name was Todd. He was brash and...so good looking. Within a few minutes of meeting him, he asked if I'd flash my tits for him."

"You're kidding!"

"Nope! He did, and I flashed. I really wanted to be with this guy. If he had asked me to suck his dick, right there on the spot, I would have been down on my knees tugging down on his zipper. I swear. He had charisma, looks, charm, and a bulge of erection all working for him as we talked. Then, when I flashed him my nips... I thought I was going to have an orgasm. It was bizarre, C. J. I was temporarily insane."

"I asked him, 'What's this?' as I touched his protruding penis -- through his jeans. He asked me if I wanted to see it and I actually had drool come out the corner of my mouth. I did want to see it."

Erica's story was getting me hotter then hell and I dropped back down where I could tongue around her shaved labia.

"Oh!" Erica exclaimed, "That's beautiful C. J., please don't stop!"

"What happened then with your Todd?"

"That's when he asked me, 'Want to come to a party with me tonight?' and he addressed me as hot-stuff."

"He had that right, Erica. You are hot, even to another woman."

"I agreed to go with him. There was no hesitation, no second thoughts. It was an immediate response to the man I wanted. Then... It was weird... I had an orgasm standing in a store with a hundred people surrounding us. I almost fainted, it was so intense."

Erica's narration was titillating and I found myself moistening to the point of leakage. I moved my pussy over her left leg and began masturbating against her shin by my own hip movement. My tongue against her clitoris was driving me manic and all this while I had handfuls of her precious breasts to play with and knead between my fingers.

Erica continued, she was breathing deep and heavy as I listened, "We met there, at the store. He was on time and, I know that I was early. We didn't drive too far before arriving at a Ramada Inn. I sat tight up against him, he smelled fresh, he had shaved smooth, I kissed him on the neck, and I knew, by touch, that he had gone erect. I wanted so badly to relieve his erection, but... Todd moved my hand aside, to keep me from tugging at his zipper, saying that we were almost there and that we were going to have one hell of a fun night; and, he called me, honey."

I was near ecstasy and experiencing small spurts of orgasmic contractions but urged her to continue, "Get to the good parts, Erica."

"Well, we were the first ones there and Todd asked me if I'd relieve him. I nodded out a smiling affirmative and we both began a wild race stripping down to nothing. Oh, his penis was huge, C.J. I reached for it as if it were the Holy Grail and as I wrapped my hand around it... Todd went into a throbbing orgasm."

I had a good visual going on in my mind as she spoke about her Todd, and when she said he went into orgasm, I entered my own, clamping down hard on Erica's ankle locked between my legs. Erica was in a heightened state and squirmed all about until she had her mouth locked onto my own clitoris in a wonton need to live the moment that she knew was upon us. God! She slurped on me like a pig emptying a trough and – IT WAS SO BEAUTIFUL a moment that I screamed out to the universe, "Futhermucking-mother-earthshaker!" and the mental fireworks of my orgasm took me out of reality for... Oh! Only God know for how long! Then, coming to my senses, I heard Erica stating...

"I swallowed it all, and he entered me, all ten inches pounded in on me. It was glorious and... I went into full-blown orgasm on his fourth, still spewing cum, thrust. That's when his two friends walked in... Without knocking!

Chapter Two

Erica and I paused our commingling, and her story recitation, to take a quick shower and get our bods ready for bed. We showered together and it was great fun for me to lather up Erica's perfect body. From personal experience, I know it is hard to allow another such an intimacy, and she did so with a perfection reserved for a master artist. She is a few years younger than I am. What a great art she had developed to be used as a pleasure giver. As I fondled her wares with my soapy hands, I worked intently to give back the wonderment she was instilling in my psyche.

When I rinsed her, squeaky clean, to my amazement, she reciprocated the lather bath as I tried with all my senses heightened into nirvana to allow her to enjoy her own play with my body. This challenged all my powers to remain passive as she soaped me front and back with a deft sensuality. I almost screamed out in ecstasy when she probed me front and backdoor with a firm determination to give me that ultimate feeling of a kinky moment.

Unable to contain my erotic nature, she forced me into an orgasmic frenzy that forced me down to the shower's marble floor in a horrific spasm of pure joy. I know this, I came close to passing out from releasing myself onto her, most assuredly, practiced manipulation of all my, seldom used, g-spots.

Erica dropped down on me as I writhed under the cascading water and found my mouth with her tasting tongue. She rinsed my flesh of any soap with gentle strokes of her hands, as she played inside my mouth, her tongue turned into an instrument of oral invigoration.

There I lay, naked, sexually exhausted, spent and yet, in a tremor of lust I wanted to reach out and touch her. We untwined our entwined bodies and shared a final rinse under the gentle pelting of the unending warm waters. We were in some zone of euphoria, we both knew this, as we both dried, each the other, in myopic vision with the fattest, softest, towels ever created, that it is lust and love that made our world spin around and around and...

My friend Donald gave us run of the house and we decided to find cookies and milk. Donald always keeps the kitchen well stocked and I knew, from past visits, exactly where the cookie jar was. We went downstairs au natural and found the Oreos with little effort.

Erica suggested we turn on the Jacuzzi and eat them there. We did. Oh! What a mess... But it was big fun and the stars were so beautiful. And when Erica smeared that dunked Oreo around my breast and sucked it off... I had to do one too! I can't remember laughing so hard with chocolate covering both of our faces. We must have looked like a real pair of freaks.

It was after midnight when we finally brushed our teeth and pulled on our matching Teddies. Mine was pale yellow, and Erica took an avocado one with a lace hem. I found it odd that putting on clothes actually heightened my libido. I wanted to play with Erica's plush body, but we had work to do.

We propped ourselves up on pillows facing each other and Erica went back to narrating her story.

Chapter Three

"Todd was in orgasm when the door opened. He pulled out of me and kneeling between my legs, said, very casually, 'Oh, oh... You guys are a little early, aren't you?'

I reached my top and covered myself...sort of. But it was too late. We were caught. Roger, the taller of the two, was carrying a bag of ice and another bag that was full of booze, which I found out just a little later, said, 'I think we need a bucket of water for you two.' He stepped around us and went into the suite. He was very cute; he had a presence and an authoritative demeanor. It should have been an embarrassing moment, but it wasn't. I think back on this now and then, and come up blank on what I thought. I gathered up the rest of my clothes and went to the bathroom with Todd following close behind me. I knew that my bare ass was being observed as I moved off; because, number 3, Gene, gave out a low cat whistle of asexual enjoyment.

Gene is extremely cute and I was happy to hear his flirty whistle. He was also carrying two bags, one of mixers and one with snacks.

Todd was apologetic to a fault while we cleaned up. I was thinking how cool it was, mainly because of the way Roger and Genie conducted their selves. It was almost as if they had planned it out ahead of time.

By the time we left the bathroom, two more guys had arrived along with 2 cases of Coors Beer. The party was underway. Oh, I was so horny, and here at my beck-and-call were all these beautiful and glowing party studs."

"Hold that thought, Erica. I need to get comfortable. Do you mind if I turn off the lights? If we open the curtains, we can enjoy the glow of the pool."

"That sounds nice, C. J. Let's do it."

Within minutes, the lights were out and the curtains hummed opened. The curtains worked by a remote control, as did the exterior pool lighting. With a little lighting tweaking, the ambiance of Donald's bedroom transformed into that of a Neptunian cave, replete with an aquacious glow that shimmered about the interior walls. It was way cool. Erica found some new wave on a Bose radio and turned the sound down to a background hum. She tossed off her teddy and laid down on her belly propping herself up with a giant feather pillow.

I laid beside her using two smaller pillows. I kept my teddy on. I held my head up with my left arm and let my right hand slide about her smooth back as she continued her story.

"More boys arrived. They were all drinking and the music became louder and louder. A lot of toasting went on, and a lot of slurred speeches were given, loudly, above the rapping group known as 50 Cent. It was crazy."

I let my hand flow down across Erica's rump... My libido was running high, yep -- on all eight cylinders. Erica's flesh is soft, and her butt -- is a thing of pure perfection. I began nipping on her back and it made me so hot.

I wanted so badly to suck on her clitoris, but she was too tender from our earlier play. My own clit was throbbing and I had to give it some invigorating touches with my free hand. I toyed with the idea of penetrating her ass – with my tongue. I was ready to move down on her when she asked if I was open for a little sucking, "Oh yes!" I demurred, and we rolled into advantageous positions amongst the sheets and pillows.

Greedily, wantonly, her mouth engulfed my mound and her tongue began a slow rotation about my erotically swollen clitoral appendage. Chills of pleasure began to erupt in my shoulders and flash-danced down my arms like bolts of lightening. I wanted to touch her back, her butt – anywhere – but our position disallowed this and it frustrated me. I wanted to play, too! With my fingers entangled in her hair, I pulled her tight into my flowing juices and entered into yet another explosive orgasm.

"Wow!" Erica screamed. "I could tell... I mean, feel you, C.J., it's simply amazing. You've got me reeling in a genuine dilemma now. I'm torn between loving a man or sleeping with a woman. You, C. J. are certainly more responsive to my own desires."

"I have been touching you in the places that I'd like to be touched. You have been very responsive, too. Now... I'm questioning my own desires. Just a minute ago, I had a strong impulse to tongue your butt crack. Although, now that I'm thinking about it, I never had a desire for someone to lick my own bottom, isn't that strange?"

Erica gave out a soft giggle, then cooed, "You certainly satisfied a few of my own desires, C.J. Like when I brought you to orgasm with my tongue, flat on your clit. I don't have sex with another woman too often. I should say, at least, not with a woman as liberal as you. That was a wonderful sensation, one that I'll not forget very soon."

"I still love a big cock as it throbs warm sperm into me during a guy's orgasm."

"Oh! Me too, C. J. That's one of God's greatest creations, hard penises throbbing at the moment of ejaculation. It's pure wonderment."

"I must agree, Erica. But it was great playing around with you. You are a very special woman."

Erica brought her mouth against mine and kissed me passionately. Our tongues darted about in an insane battle to taste more than the other one. We embraced in a loving hug of mutual understanding that what had happened, and what was happening, was a one-time fling. It was not a capitulation into abject lesbianism; but a night of sexual fantasy brought to fruition, or rather...orgasm, for sure.

"My story seems insignificant now; actually it's trite as we lay here. I don't want to tell you any more of it, OK?"

We snuggled then... It was nice. We didn't talk for the longest while. The music was so soft in the background that sleep overtook us both. Neither of us had any concept of time. It was an insignificant element to two, too exhausted lovers (I think this is the first time I ever saw all those 2 words in a row...).

Donald arrived around eight the next morning. He flew in from Japan, and then drove from the San Francisco airport another five hours up to Tahoe. He was staggering as he entered the bedroom and began to strip.

"Is there enough room for me in there?" he chided. "I'll be asleep in a two count."

Erica never moved, never woke at all, as Donald moved in between us. The weary traveler was right, he was asleep before my hand finished a 720 over his six-pack. I pulled a sheet over his nudity and went away to get some coffee brewing.

As for Erica's story, she never did finish telling me about her L.A. night with the three boys. Now... I can't wait until I hear her story about waking up naked -- with Donald next to her.

"Oh! Life holds so many dilemmas."

The End!

Hot Desking Stories

Hot Desking I

Hi, my name is C. J. Starr and my friend Kortney just left my house radiant like a bride and I'm going to tell you how she got that glow…

Hot Desking is when companies are too cheap to allow employees their own desks. But here's the deal, hot desking didn't get that name for nothing, little do people know that the origins of the term, "hot desking" came from the story I'm about to tell you… This is Kortney's story, and I'm retelling it here with her full permission…

The company my friend Kortney works for took a hit with the economy so they made some cutbacks and moved to a smaller office, some people not only had to share offices but they had to share desks. People ended up "hot desking."

Kortney worked an early morning to afternoon shift. Being in the financial sector, she liked being up early with the stock market, and it meant getting home in time for a vibrant afternoon.

Kortney had a desk drawer for her things, with a lock, and the person who shared her desk had another drawer with a separate lock and key. The desk was always clean when she went into work. She thought at first that it would suck not having her own space, but it didn't take long to get used to the idea. Other than not working the typical nine to five, the hot desking seemed to be working out better than she thought it would. She particularly liked getting to take off early on Fridays. It made the weekend seem longer.

So a few months passed without incident, until the day she went to work like every other day but by the time she left work her life had changed forever.

The day started out typical enough, she got to the office and, followed her ritualistic routine, first putting away her purse in her desk drawer when she noticed that her hot desking partner's desk drawer was unlocked and open. She opened the drawer quickly, peeked inside, then shut it, and went into the coffee room to get some coffee.

Setting her coffee cup on her desk, she thought about whether she should open the desk drawer again. She knew nothing about her desk partner except that they always left the area clean, left no telltale signs of who they were or what kind of life they led. She glanced around to make sure no one was watching and opened the drawer quickly. Damn. Nothing. Pushing aside rubber bands, paper clips, she didn't know what she was looking for or hoping to find, but there was nothing of interest until she pushed some note papers aside and saw a Kindle. She took it out of the drawer and noticed that the name on it read, "Kiki." Hmmm. So the person is a woman that I "hot desk" with… Wonder what kind of books she reads? Skimming through the titles, she stopped at the one that read, Seducing the Boss. Sounded interesting. Skipping around the pages, she immediately became aroused at the vividly written description of two kissing and licking and sucking each other into oblivion.

A flushed Kortney slipped the Kindle into her purse and counted the minutes until lunch. When her lunch break came she hurried to the park across the street from the office building to read more. She was surprised she'd been so turned on by the female on female lovemaking but it aroused her in a way she liked!

She ended up spending her lunch hour, and every free moment she could that afternoon at work, reading. She felt her panties moisten and the twitching in her vagina was itching for relief. She thought about racing to the bathroom to finish herself off but she decided the fantasy of women would best wait until she was in the safe confines of her own bedroom at home where she could spread her legs, get out her vibrator, and really let loose.

When she got home, she poured herself a chilled glass of Chardonnay, removed her clothes until she was deliciously naked, and slipped in between her silk sheets.

Kortney envisioned two women making love. She thought about the characters in the story licking each other's pussies, their breasts pressed against bodies, nipples erect. She fantasized that she would end up in a woman's arms, her warm embrace… The thoughts were turning her on until she was about to explode with unbridled sexuality that needed immediate satisfaction. She grabbed the vibrator, sucked on it, and then ran it through her wet folds. She thrust it in her waiting cunt and grasped her breast with the other. Writhing on the bed, given over to the fantasy. She wanted to be with a woman, being licked by a longhaired beauty until she came.

At work the next day her boss dropped off a stack of reports and spreadsheets for her to work on. It would mean staying late so she went down to the coffee shop at street level, ordered a double latte, and headed back to the office.

Her normal quitting time came and went, and she still had a lot of work to get finished. All the others on her shift left the building, and the cleaning crew that prepared the building between shifts came in. Kortney worked through that. Even the regular nine to five execs had left for the day.

Many of the second shifters didn't even come in on Fridays, she knew, opting for the more cost-effective four-day workweek, so she didn't really expect to see anyone.

So Kortney was surprised to hear a woman's voice. It was soft and tempting, "Hello..."

She looked to see a dark-haired Asian beauty. Kortney's nipples tightened and her vagina moistened.

"I'm Kiki," she said with a sultry seduction. "That's my desk."

"It's my desk too," Kortney said, standing, offering her hand, her legs shaking, her inner thighs throbbing. "I'm Kortney."

"You have soft hands," Kiki said as she held Kortney's hands and then caressed the back, running her fingers down the length of her fingers.

Kortney immediately dropped her hand and stepped away, fantasy was one thing, but this was a little too real.

"Do you want to know why I love working the late shift on Fridays, Kortney?" Kiki held up a ring of keys and jangled them in front of her face.

Kortney grinned, instantly curious.

"Follow me, and I'll show you..." Kiki was wearing a short skirt and had long legs, which Kortney wanted desperately to stroke and caress.

Kortney followed the dark haired beauty out into the corridor and a door, which Kortney thought might be a storage closet.

"I got these keys at the last holiday party."

Kiki slipped a key into the doorknob and unlocked it quickly. "I got this special key from a special exec on the Board of Directors."

"Mr. Baxter?" Kiki asked curiously.

"No, Mrs." She holds a spot on the Board and she secretly holds a liking for me. She gave me this key so we could meet in private."

"Might we be expecting her?"

"Oh, no, not tonight, she's out of town. I hang onto the key for my own personal use."

Kortney thought she should turn around and run. Whatever she was getting into couldn't be good. She was breaching security, there probably were cameras everywhere, and she'd probably get fired.

"Come on," Kiki said as she raised her finger to Kortney.

Kortney knew she wanted the gesture to be suggestive, and it was, it totally turned her on and she thought she might explode. She thought about how hot and tight her pussy would feel wrapped around Kiki's finger.

They stepped inside the executive lounge. The poshness of it blew Kortney away. Leather chairs, cut crystal carafes of fine liquor. One entire wall was a walk-in humidor filled with cigars.

"Want something to drink?" Kiki asked. "Rum? Wine? Champagne?"

"Anything," she said, crossing to one of the large leather chairs. Kiki poured a drink and handed to Kortney. She couldn't ignore that glint in her eye...

Kortney sipped the bubbly champagne. Soon the glass was empty and her head was spinning. Her mind was filling with images of Kiki between her thighs, sucking on her clit, and fingering her pussy. A small moan escaped her lips. "I have to tell you," Kortney began. "You left your desk drawer open the other day and..."

"You read my Kindle, didn't you?"

She nodded and felt a hot blush burn her cheeks.

"I bet I know which story you read."

"Oh?" Kortney was feeling so embarrassed but she was so excited at the same time. She loved the story of the women making love but she didn't think it was something she could ever admit.

"What did you think?"

She wanted to tell her everything in a gush, but held back.

"I bet you read Seducing the Boss?" Kiki said.

Kortney nodded, "Yes," she whispered.

"I get horny too. For breaks on Friday nights, I come in here, fix myself a drink, and fuck myself with my fingers right here in that very chair that you're sitting in." Her words lowered to a whisper as she told Kortney this, and she leaned over the chair, tickling her ear with her breath. "It will be much more fun to fuck you." Then without missing a beat, Kiki ran her fingers up Kortney's thighs, under her skirt, until she found the edge of her lacy underwear. She pulled them off in an instant and tossed them across the room in a dramatic moment of pure lust. Then she slipped her skirt off and threw it aside.

"Spread your legs," Kiki commanded as she quickly stripped off her own clothes.

Kortney obliged and felt her flesh squeak against the leather chair beneath her as she moved her hips forward to give Kiki better tongue access. Whatever she'd gotten herself into, there was no stopping now. She couldn't stop if she wanted to, this was a fantasy come true and she was going to savor every fucking moment of it.

Kortney decided to be helpful (actually she was about to come and she wanted Kiki to not suck her dry but suck her tits too) so she unbuttoned her top, revealing her voluptuous breasts. Kortney wanted her breasts in her mouth, but wanted her mouth on her clit more. She wanted it both, she wanted it all…

Kortney daringly lowered her head between Kiki's thighs, flicking her tongue, and lapping at her bud. Chills coursed through her body. Just as she'd imagined, she delved two fingers into her cunt, and while she did, she reached up and played with her own nipple.

"I want to taste you…"

Kiki laid on the plush rug. Kortney took a moment to admire Kiki's body. Her creamy skin and lush curves completely turned her on. Kortney dove in and lapped inside and around Kiki's pussy. She'd never tasted anything sweeter than Kiki's love tunnel. Her tongue, lips, and fingers worked furiously at her pussy. This was the moment she'd waited for her entire life. Any love making she'd had before this moment was just sex. This for Kortney was more than sex, this was lovemaking, but it was more than lovemaking, it was like she'd been freed into a new life she always only dreamed and fantasized about. This was real; this was pleasure to the ninth degree. This was going to be a new life for her.

Kiki and Kortney had a mutual exchange of pleasuring each other with equal tenderness. Soon their tenderness moved into ferocious sexual screaming as they entered orgasm each licking the other with unbridled passion.

The women spent the rest of the evening caressing each other, and napping in each other's arms. Before Kortney left, Kiki leaned in and gave her the most delicious, salacious long lasting kiss Kortney had ever experienced. She didn't know if it was the alcohol or from her first real orgasm, but Kortney felt like she had been reborn and she liked the way it felt…

Hot Desking II

Intro: Once upon a time, two sexual girls shared a desk at work in a cost-cutting endeavor entitled, "Hot Desking." These two girls worked different shifts until one day their paths crossed at work and low and behold, they soon became at-work lovers. Their names are Kiki and Kortney and their story was told in the City Girl Series Quickie Read, "Hot Desking" but if you missed it, no worries, you can go back and buy it anywhere ebooks are sold and catch up, but for now, here's the sequel... Enjoy!

Love, C. J. Starr

"Well, hell," I said as I flopped into one of the fancy executive chairs and sucked on the end of a cigar I had no intention of smoking. I wished I had a cock in my mouth instead right now, but I had to settle.

Kiki sat down across from me and put her stockinged feet up on the coffee table between us. She held a glass of scotch. The executives never knew we kept skimming off the top because we refilled the bottle with a little water each time.

I really hated Valentine's Day. During my entire shift, men with deliveries of balloons, chocolates, and huge floral arrangements had come and gone. All the single girls, and most of the marrieds, had something from their sweetheart by the end of the workday.

"Jealous much, Kortney?" Kiki asked me after taking a long sip of her scotch.

I shrugged. "You didn't get anything either."

She'd switched her shift and now had the cubicle next to mine. We still snuck in to use the executive "washroom" after everyone else left, though. We felt like we deserved it after what we went through here at the job.

"What should we do to change that?"

"We could always just fool around here."

Kiki sat forward, spread her legs, and pushed her skirt up. I could see she had no panties under the well-tailored, designer threads. Her pussy glistened in the mood lighting of the room.

She touched herself then, and my pussy clenched in response. I could feel the panties I wore, and now wish I didn't -- dampen as she brushed her finger repeatedly over her big clit.

"Are you going to just sit over there and be a cunt tease?" I asked, swinging my legs down off the edge of the chair and spreading them for her.

She nearly leaped across the coffee table to get at me. Eagerly she pulled my panties down and, literally, dove into my muff.

She was insatiable, eating out my pussy like a starving man on Thanksgiving would attack a sweet potato pie.

I hitched one leg over the arm of the chair, giving her even more access to my goodies. Her tongue and fingers went crazy against me, driving me to climax before I could even beg her to slow down, to make it last.

I squirted for her, drenching her face and the chair with my cum.

She pulled away, giggling, and used one of the fine linen hand towels left for the executives to clean herself off. Then she threw the towel at me so I could mop my juices off the chair.

"So now what?" she asked, once I'd tossed the towel into a discreet hamper and returned. "Go find a guy and hold a gun to his head until he buys us some flowers?" Kiki and I played a lot, but we were by no means a couple, and each of us hoped to find someone special and permanent.

"The first part sounds good," Kiki told me.

"Find a guy?" I asked.

"Sure. Why not?" She tipped her head back and looked at the ceiling. "Where should we go?"

"Where would all the hot single guys be on Valentine's Day?"

Oddly, the idea seemed to come to us at the same time. "Basketball!"

We jumped up, poured the scotch back into the bottle, and I put the cigar I hadn't even lit back into the humidor with the others. On our way down, Kiki used her smartphone to buy us two courtside seats.

In the back of a cab, we tried our best to go from that day-at-the-office look to ravish-us-please. We definitely didn't want to be late for tip-off, though, so stopping by either of our apartments was out of the question. We combed each other's hair out with our fingers, trying to style them into tousled locks. We took off our jackets and undid the top few buttons of our blouses, and hiked our skirts up just a smidge. The cab driver kept watching us in the rear-view mirror, and despite how cold it was outside, the cab's interior seemed steamy and hot, probably due in large part to Kiki's and my transformation.

The driver let us out in front of the arena, and we made it to our seats just in time tip-off. Waiters brought us wine and snacks as the game progressed, and Kiki and I got a little rambunctious, embracing enthusiastically when our team scored a point. In fact, I think we became something of a distraction to some of the players.

The game, however, as I understand it was a "shoot-out" meaning the lead kept switching back and forth, never with more than a few points between them. We stayed glued to our seats until the end, when the final buzzer went off while a shot was still in the air. The ball went in the hoop, and our team won by two.

Kiki and I jumped up, hugged, and screamed. I'd never gone to a game before, but I could see why people loved it. The excitement, all the hot guys running back and forth, muscles rippling under taut skin. They converted me to a season ticket holder right then and there.

As Kiki and I prepared to leave, one of the ushers in a burgundy jacket and an earpiece like a Secret Service agent approached us.

"The Duke would like to see you two ladies if you have the time."

For a moment, I thought he meant a real duke, like some English royalty had attended the game or something, but Kiki nudged me in the ribs and said, "He means the Duke of Dunks!"

Oh, Terrell Doucette. I sure knew that name after watching the game. He was our power center, and definitely earned the title he had.

Giggling, we stood and followed the usher into the bowels of the arena. Down a dimly lit corridor, through glass doors that opened automatically, emblazoned with the team's logo, and then into...

Oh my God.

The locker room.

I'd never seen so much hot, glistening man meat in all my life. My panties dampened in an instant. Kiki grabbed my arm, but I couldn't tell if it was out of trepidation or joy.

The players, in various states of undress, surrounded us. Massive cocks of all shades hung heavy between men's legs as they showered, toweled off, or dressed.

I'm sure my jaw hung slack as I took it all in. Sure, I loved pussy, but a girl needs her twat filled by some real, hot rods of passion sometimes too, and I would welcome any of these.

But the usher had brought us here for just one man, and I hoped that he wanted us for the reason I expected, not to chew us out for distracting the players with our D-cup breasts on the sidelines.

The usher led us through the valleys of glorious flesh until he finally stopped in front of one particular locker area. It sat slightly apart from the others, and a massive man stood in front of it, his back to us. I took a moment to follow all the lines of his muscles and how they cut in at his waist. He already had on a pair of tighty-whities, and boy were they ever! I wanted to just grab one of those tight globes and take a bite out of it.

He resembled some primordial god, gleaming and dark skinned, towering over the rest of us. I would certainly sacrifice myself to him! He turned then, and I got a faceful of his junk. Hell, it was practically at eye level.

I licked my lips, and raised my gaze to meet his. Sparks lit between us.

"These the girls?" he asked the usher, and at the sound of his voice, Kiki moaned and pressed more weight against me.

"Yes, sir," the usher said.

I thought I could jump him right then, but I realized he probably had something better in mind.

Terrell smiled big at the two of us. "Hello, ladies. You two really seemed to enjoy the game."

"Oh yeah," Kiki said. She pushed off me and took a wobbly step forward. She reached up and stroked a hand down Terrell's chest, across his tight abs, and to the waistband of his underwear. She gave it a playful snap. Gazing up at him, she said, "You really know how to handle balls, don't you?"

I couldn't help but giggle.

"You can go," Terrell said with a dismissive wave of his hand to the usher. The other man turned and left.

Around us, the other players dressed and departed the locker room, but it seemed as if we were in our own little world, cut off from everyone around us.

I wanted to touch too, so I joined Kiki in running my hands over Terrell's body. He leaned down and kissed me, then Kiki.

Soon, we were all heavy petting each other, a knot of bodies standing there, learning the planes of each other's skin.

"Hey!" someone yelled from across the room.

Kiki and I stepped back and looked toward the newcomer.

"The assistant coach," Terrell murmured to us.

"Post game press conference," the coach barked.

"Can't you see I'm busy?" Terrell said, and I felt his hand on my ass, cupping it possessively.

"Now, or take a fine."

Terrell sighed. "Care to join me, ladies?"

Kiki and I nodded and we three headed off for the conference. When Terrell said, "Join me," I thought he'd just meant in the room, but I was way wrong. He brought us up, one on each side, to the draped table at the front, and we all sat down at the microphones. I couldn't believe it. Cameras flashed like lightning and people shouted, "Duke!" or "Terrell, over here!" and "Mr. Doucette, just one question!" The whole scene made me fell like a star. I waved with crooked fingers at some of the journalists.

Terrell began answering questions, but I didn't care about the team's chances for the play-offs or the opposing coach's defensive strategy. I wanted to get out of there and get on with the evening. I decided I would remind him, so I reached a hand under the table, slid it up his thigh, and...

Someone's hand was already stroking his crotch! I shot a look down the table at Kiki, and she smiled back at me, a wicked glint in her eye.

Together we worked him through the fabric of his expensive pants. As we did, his answers slowly became more hesitant and less articulate. When he started to squirm a little in his seat, he finally declared, "That's enough for tonight," and pulled us to our feet. We headed out another door, down a corridor, and out into the night air. There, a limo waited. The driver, leaning against the side and reading the paper, quickly moved to open doors and usher us inside.

Kiki and I sat on one of the long, plush seats of the limo while Terrell sat on the other. He closed the smoky glass between the driver, and us and then smiled in the dim lights of the limo.

"So I haven't seen you ladies at a game before." He leaned forward, his elbows on his knees. "And believe me, I would have noticed."

"We didn't have any plans for Valentine's Day, so we decided to have a girls' night."

"So is there room for a guy in all that?" He waved a hand toward us.

Kiki and I exchanged glances. "I don't know," I said. "What do you think, Kiki?"

Kiki fiddled with the top button of her blouse and leaned in toward me. "We are awfully...close." She brushed a kiss across my lips.

"It can be awfully...hard to get between us," I wrapped my arms around her and pulled our bodies together. I loved the feel of her breasts trapped against me, her nipples so hard they nearly poked right through her lacy bra and blouse.

"And I don't really know that I need I guy, because Kortney here is really good at eating pussy."

She pushed me down, and I took the hint. I kneeled on the floor of the limo and reached up under Kiki's skirt. I found the waistband of her skimpy panties and pulled them down, then threw them across the limo to Terrell. He caught them in one hand, and then brought them up to his face. He inhaled, and I pushed the hem of Kortney's skirt up to her waist, revealing her shaved and already damp pussy for Terrell's perusal. He lowered the panties from his face, but kept them clutched in his hand. I pushed Kiki's legs farther apart, and then dove in. I licked and lapped, enjoying the sweet, cloying taste of her. Before long, I had her squirming, and I could hear Terrell moaning and masturbating behind me.

I couldn't watch him, my head buried as it was between Kiki's legs, but I imagined him as I ate her out. I pictured his huge, dark cock in his hands, the massive paws that could palm a basketball working him closer and closer to the edge.

Kiki came, screaming, and I sat up and wiped my mouth. I turned to look at Terrell, and just as I did, he came, spurting jets of cum over the front of his unzipped trousers.

He cleaned himself off with a towel from the minibar and sat up, then refastened his pants. "Nice show," he said. "I think I've figured out a way to make this all work. I won't try to get between the two of you, but how about under?"

The limo pulled to a stop and the door opened. Terrell led us through the front door of a very ritzy place and to a private elevator. We traveled up to the penthouse, and Terrell immediately pulled us into his bedroom.

Soft jazz already played, and a fire burned in his fireplace. A huge white fur throw covered the bed, and I couldn't wait to feel its softness against my skin.

While Kiki and I explored the opulent flat, Terrell went and rinsed himself off, then came back with a towel, hardly bigger than a washcloth, wrapped around his middle.

"I thought you girls would be naked by now," he said, and stripped away his towel. Kiki squealed and clapped her hands. I just whistled in appreciation.

Then our clothes came off, and we all dove for the bed.

At first, we formed a tangle of limbs as we explored each other, learning the taste of flesh, the planes of skin, and the bend of limb. Then Terrell reminded us what he wanted, and after he sheathed himself with a condom from the bedside table, he lay on the bed.

"I want to fuck Kiki first, while you sit on my face," he told me. I had no problem agreeing. Soon, Kiki was riding his cock like a rodeo cowboy, and Terrell's tongue was buried in my snatch. Kiki had her hands on my breasts, and mine held onto her hips for dear life. We kissed, biting, licking, and becoming completely lost in the over-the-top extravagance of the fucking.

We all three came in a loud cacophony of orgasms, and then collapsed in a heap on the bed.

After a break, a shower, and a snack, we went at it again. This time, Terrell fucked me.

After, we all fell asleep.

In the middle of the night, though, I woke up to the wet sounds of more lovemaking. I opened my gritty eyes to see Kiki sucking Terrell's huge cock. God, she was insatiable! His hands held her hair in a thick rope, and his hips pushed up spastically as she ran her lips up and down the length of his cock.

I didn't want to interrupt, but the scene had me hot in a shot. I dove my fingers into my own cunt and fucked myself as I watched. Kiki, always one to want everyone happy, reached up and pinched one of my nipples. The feeling shot straight to my clit, and I came.

Then we all fell asleep again.

Early the next morning, Kiki and I crept out of the fancy building and into the cold February air. Terrell hadn't even woken up as we left. Holding hands, we headed down the street to the subway, practically skipping.

"I can't believe we did that," I said. Now, without some very carefully executed and timed preparations, we'd both be late for work.

"It was so hot," Kiki said. "We have to do this again!"

"Totally," I said.

Then we passed a flower vendor on the sidewalk, and a wave of melancholy swept through me. "We didn't get flowers, even after all that," I said, pouting.

Kiki pulled to a halt, turned back to the vendor, and bought the largest bouquet of red roses he had. With a flourish, she handed them to me. I pulled the finest of the bunch out and tucked it behind Kiki's ear. She smiled, and then we embraced and kissed. Kiki's tongue pushed passed my lips, and mine met hers. We licked and swiped. I could feel her nipples pebbling beneath her shirt.

"We never got your underwear back," I whispered into her mouth. It probably got left in the limo.

"Then we'd better find me some fast, or else I'm going to be dripping pussy juice down the street. You get me so turned on, Kortney."

I heard a few whistles around us and, smiling, finally pushed away. "We'd better hurry." I pulled her toward the stairs to the subway. "My apartment is closer. We'll go there. I'm sure I'll have something that will fit you."

With that, we descended the stairs, and headed for home.

The End!

Christmas Menage

Chapter One

I received this email from a friend of mine who has agreed that I may share it with you. Xo, CJ Starr.

Dear C. J.,

You know how you said one should be open to new ideas, well a friend of mine told me this story, and I wanted to share it with you. It happened over Winter Break.

It was an unusually cold December; snow had piled up a good foot around town. There was a spattering of holiday decorations lighting up the evening as Kiki daydreamed while looking out her apartment window. She had decided to stay at school for the holidays. Actually, truth be told her grades needs boosting. It started snowing again and she put away her books. She felt like her college town was a ghost town until after the New Year, at least, at the popular spots. She picked up her roommate's December issue of Penthouse, and began paging Britney's sexy magazine.

She was naked, playfully flicking on her clit to the arty centerfold, when the phone rang. It was Britney, "Hey Kiki, it's me, Britney. How's it going there?"

"Great!" she lied; she was totally bored. "I'm getting a lot of work done. There's no one around."

"I figured. That's why I'm calling. I'm toying with the idea of coming back, tonight...if I can get a flight."

"What's up with that? I thought you were with cutesy Meg and her parents." She immediately realized she may have sounded sarcastic. She changed the subject. "Didn't it snow? You're up in Aspen, right?" She sensed her jealousy but tried to hide it.

"Ah... The lodge is full and the snow's great; but I had a big fight with Meg. I pretty much told her to kiss my ass...in front of her parents." She let out a barrel laugh. "Can you pick me up at the airport?"

"No problem. What time?"

"Midnight. The last flight out of Denver. If I miss this flight, I'm screwed until tomorrow."

"OK. I'll be there, Brit."

"Thank you so much, sweetie!" There was a short pause, and then Britney added a soft, "Love you!" And the connection went silent.

That tender, spoken, "Love you" sent an electrified current humming down through Kiki's entire body. She laid down on her bed and envisioned Britney's perfect body. She has the smallest ass, by far the cutest ass on campus. Her breasts are full and she dresses to show her "endowments" with a hint, no...a distinct nuance of slut! Her areoles are small and dark, and every time Kiki saw them...they protruded thimble-sized nipples. It's, as if, she has no concept of how titillating, or of how sexual she naturally is.

Kiki's clitoris enlarged under her soft fingers and her thoughts drifted to taking one of Britney's breasts into her mouth and sucking on it like there was no tomorrow. Then she envisioned Britney stepping out of the shower and envisioned her beautifully shaved pubic hair with its small dark heart-shaped tuft just above her pussy.

Her mouth watered and she swore; she was salivating! Kiki increased her circular massage, rewarding herself with pleasure, and began to feel the moisture ooze between her pussy lips. A wave of passion arched through her pelvis and she pressed down on her clit to heighten the spontaneous moment of a solo orgasm. She (mentally) buried her tongue deep into Britney as she protruded her tongue out from her own mouth. It was at that moment that she heard her own voice, screaming out, "Oh! Britney!" and Kiki's body stiffened…like the cock on a jock in a crowded, all girls' shower.

She, still breathing heavy, entered a steamy shower. It was going on six and she knew it would take a good hour to drive to the airport. Time was going to run out, very quick. But, she had this wonderful sense of excitement going on inside of her. She had made up her mind…she was going to hook up with her Britney, soon!

She looked out at the falling snow. It was really coming down hard, reducing visibility to almost nothing. That's when she decided she wanted the evening to be beyond special. Kiki looked up a number for a rental car service.

"Hello! You've reached Ames Livery Service, Happy Holidays!"

"What's chance of me getting a limo…just to the airport, and back?"

"Do you have an account with us?"

"No. But I'm a big tipper." Kiki let out a nervous laugh.

"All of our cars are booked and in service." Jenny lied; she just wanted to get the hell out there. She was tired of the phones ringing all day, and besides, she had to pick up some beer and smokes for her girlfriend before she got home.

"Please, I really need a car. I want to surprise my girlfr…" Kiki stopped herself. What was she thinking, Britney was not her girlfriend, she was her roommate, but girlfriend, no. She was the one she fantasized about, the one she got off to, but girlfriend. Wishful thinking. "You know what…" Her voice started to crack. "Umm. Never mind."

"Wait a second…we've just had a cancellation." Jenny lied, again. There was something about this girl's demeanor, a note of desperation, and it made her sound sexually intriguing.

"Oh my God! Thank you so much." Kiki verged on tears, "I'll make it worth your while!"

"No problem. Just give me your address, and I'll be there." Jenny felt a wave of euphoria enshroud her; it was as if Christmas Cupid or something had hit her. There was an uncanny, yummy feeling about helping out a girl in need, a feeling that appealed right into her very soul. She called home and announced that she would be, "…late."

The driver, Jenny, arrived at Kiki's apartment at 10 o'clock sharp, just as agreed.

"Hey! Know what? Come sit up front with me." Jenny graciously opened the door for Kiki.

Kiki sat down and took Jenny in. She was quite interesting. First up, 'cause she was a female limo driver. Second, 'cause she was dressed in a black suit, and kid you not, she even had on a black driver's cap, a chauffeur's cap, and wore a man's black tie. She looked hot.

On their way to the airport, Kiki glanced back into the main part of the limo, and saw an interior lined with white twinkling lights and a fake candle glowing in the cabin, and there was a bottle of champagne chilling in a silver ice bucket.

By the time they arrived at the airport, Kiki didn't know what got into her, but she had poured out her heart to the driver on how much she was in love with Britney. Jenny was completely understanding and sympathetic with her need.

Britney's flight was on time, despite the snow. Kiki met her at the baggage claim and almost died when she made her appearance from the inner concourse. She looked so hot. She looked like a goddess. Her long dark hair contrasted with the white coat she was wearing which had a hint of fur around the collar. Her cheeks were rosy and her skin seemed to glow. Her smooth approach was all smiles and when they hugged, she kissed Kiki, full-lipped on her mouth. It was her first, on the lips, kiss from a girl; except for once…at a party, but that's another story.

This split-second kiss seemed to last an eternity and left Kiki wanting, needing, more. It was a beautiful moment and she could feel love explode all around the humming carousel. A warm embrace followed their kiss. They hugged long and dear, that is…until Jenny, the driver, interrupted, "Ready?"

The three of them got into the car. Kiki didn't know if it was the excitement at the thought of having Britney back all to herself for the holidays or what, but she was getting more aroused every minute.

Britney took off her jacket as Kiki poured her a glass of champagne. "It's really good to see you, Brit." She couldn't help it, her voice gushed, and she knew that she couldn't hide her desires any longer. "Brit, I have something to tell you."

Brit swirled her index finger in the champagne glass and methodically licked her finger dry. "Yes, doll?" Her voice was like velvet. She was like an imaginary playmate come to life. And she was all Kiki's.

"Driver," Britney said as she tapped on closed window partition.

Jenny opened the glass, "Yes?"

"It's a little warm back here."

"I see that…" Jenny had been orgasmic since she first set eyes on this wonder. She'd been orgasmic since she first saw Kiki. Hell, she'd been orgasmic since she first heard

Kiki's desperate voice on the phone, one of needing an orgasm that only a woman can deliver. "I'll adjust the thermostat." Damn, Jenny hated the way she sounded so matter-of-fact. Where was her sense of spontaneity?

"Thanks." Britney shut the partition and curled up next to Kiki. "What is it darling?"

"I just wanted you to know how I feel." Kiki leaned toward Britney and kissed her soft and tenderly on the lips. "Damn, you taste good!"

Britney let out a thunderous laugh. "Girlfriend, come here." She pulled no punches, wasted no time. She took another sip of champagne, set the glass down, and moved in towards Kiki's waiting self. Pulling off Kiki's shirt, she caressed her breasts with her hands and licked her face around the lips.

Jenny knew the threshold had been crossed. Yes, the window to the back cabin was closed, but that didn't stop drivers from knowing what was going on back there. Her juices were flowing and almost as soon as she pulled onto the freeway, she decided to make a detour. "Do you all feel like something to eat?"

"Mmmm," Kiki let out an, "Uh huh…" But she wasn't really sure if she spoke or not, and why was their driver talking to her. No. Not now…not when she was so close to having her roommate become her lover, she said, "Whatever."

Jenny pulled into McDonald's parking lot. She partially opened the window and peered in on her passengers. The women were laying on the seat kissing and had their legs intertwined. "Anybody care for a hot chocolate?"

Kiki helped Britney out of her pants. She wasn't wearing panties, and when she slid the pants out from under her butt, she fully exposed Britney's beautiful pussy. "Oops!" Kiki laughed.

"You can come back here for some champagne, if you'd like," Britney said to Jenny.

Britney toyed with Kiki's hair, curling it around her finger. "You don't mind, do you doll?"

Kiki was pretty much in seventh heaven and so excited, this was all new to her, and she was open to new ideas and she wasn't about to stop the flow of action. "Sure! Whatever you like."

"Uhh, we've gotten into a bit of nasty weather," Jenny said into the car's radio. "I won't be back, until late. Merry Christmas, eh!"

Jenny hopped into the backseat. Parked in the shadows of an empty parking lot. With the darkened limo windows, no one could see what was going on inside. Although, Jenny would not have minded, even if they could.

"Well, aren't you the formal one." Britney said as she began to remove Jenny's tie. Britney was wearing a tight sweater that amply showed off her bosom and Jenny placed hands on each of them deliciously savoring each stroke against her soft flesh.

Jen quickly removed her own shirt after Brit took off her uniform tie. Jen has a boyish flat chest. Britney, in the dim lighting, momentarily thought that Jen actually was a boy. With Kiki's tongue darting into her, Britney dug a hand down the front of Jen's pants searching for a cock.

Britney had a brief moment of disappointment, but her excitement tripled when she slit her fingers up into the begging wetness of Jen's open pussy. Jen reached Brit's mouth with her tongue penetrating wetly into a passionate face fuck. Brit wantonly returned the invasion and the moans of individual ecstasy filled the black leathered sanctuary.

Shedding the remainder of their clothes enhanced their frolicking. Jen wished aloud that she wanted a cock, a real dick, one which she could fuck her new friends with, and stick it up their asses.

"I have a ten inch one, but it's in my luggage." Teased Britney.

A muffled plea came out of Kiki's busy mouth that was sucking tight on Britney's cunt, "O get et." She managed to say.

Jen asked if it was a strap-on, then offered, "I'll go get it. Which bag is it in?" and began pulling her driver pants on.

"The small beige one. It's right on top in a plastic case."

Kiki came up for air and snuggled into Britney's side, all the while keeping a caressing hand rubbing across Brit's firm belly. With her free hand, Kiki reached a protruding nipple that had popped forth from Jen's boyish chest. Jen stopped pulling up a boot and bent in to French kiss Kiki's succulent mouth. Their tongues met and Kiki's arm left Britney's stomach and quickly encircled Jen's still naked top.

Kiki pulled her head back, and exclaimed, "You can't go out there, Jen. You'll freeze!"

Jen slipped into the driver jacket against the caring protests, "I'll only be a sec…" and she was out the door. The cold rush of air and a few errant snowflakes felt marvelous to the girls. Rubbing steam-buildup from the rear window, they watched Jen from their kneeling positions on warm leather seat.

Britney asked, "Kiki, I really want this girl to pack my ass with the dildo, do you mind if I get it first? I sense that she likes you more, but I really need this, OK?"

"Oh Britney, honey. I'll help her all the way," and they smiled at each the other with Christmassy glow as the trunk lid slammed closed.

Jen dashed into the cabin with a blast Iowa wind at her chauffer heels, "Got it!" Holding the case high like a trophy won at a NASCAR race. Britney was shaking as she raised her ass in anticipation of the now chocolate lubricated rubber penis. Jen had stripped and readied (positioned and tightened the straps) dildo faster than one of Santa's flying reindeer. Kiki moisten Brit's perky hole with her tongue while grasping Jen's butt for stability.

Jen was not gentle as she forced the cock's head into Brit's ass. Britney yelped in pleasure with the insertion, it was more like squeak, one that shortened to a series of ee, ee, ees…as Jen pushed the ribbed rod all the way in with a full bodied thrust.

Jen, like an overtly horny man, entered into a solo, premature orgasm. Jen, sensing this orgasm, frantically, pulled Kiki to her mouth and – in a frenzy of sexual lust, entered her own orgasm with the dildo stuck firm, up her contracting butt cheeks and squeezing down hard on rubber the cock.

Kiki, a virgin to sex toys, was floating in a euphoric mental state akin to Nirvana when her friends went ballistic. Somehow, Jen managed to reach Kiki's pussy and insert her thin fingers firmly on her, beginning to throb, clitoris. Kiki went up into the Milky Way on an orgasmic surge that would render most mere mortals unconscious. With an air of mystic acknowledgement, the three sexually exhausted adventurers wished each other, Merry Christmas, with deep breaths of erotic recovery.

Epilogue

OK, C. J., That's my story... Love you!

To all my friends out there... This is my Holiday Quickie Read, and I'm C. J. Starr. Here's wishing you all a very happy holiday, and a very, very orgasmic Christmas!

With Love, C. J. Starr.

A Special Note from C. J. Starr

Thank you so much for reading this story! I hope you enjoyed it as much as I did. Sex is the best, now go get a good rest and prepare yourself to read more of my delicious City Girl Series quickie reads. Hey, visit my website too at cjstarr.net. xoxo, CJ Starr.

About the Author

C. J. Starr is the bestselling author of the City Girl Series. These quickie reads are about women with high ambition and libido to match. C. J. Starr writes great sex!

List of City Girl Series

Women Rock (a compilation)
Santa Girl
Indy Girl
Cream Star
Cock for Sale
Horny Harold
Kellie's Bike Ride
Welcome Home Ménage
Easter Best
Lucky Leprecock
Hot Desking 2
Bondage Bunny
Private Fitting
Christmas Ménage
Dabbing in Oils
Igor and the Count
Trick or Eat Me
Hot Desking
Cassandra's Independence
Mardi Gras Ménage
Summer Heat
An Insatiable Christmas Gift
Erica's Dilemma
My Name is CJ Starr and These R My Stories, Vol. 2
Aloha
Spring Me
Valentine
Play Date

My Name is CJ Starr and These R My Stories, Vol. 1
April
Vassar Girl
Seducing the Boss
Nowhere to Turn
Housemates

New Line Press.com

C. J. Starr

2041088R00048

Printed in Great Britain
by Amazon.co.uk, Ltd.,
Marston Gate.